JORINDA AND JORINGEL

by the
Brothers Grimm
Retold by
David Cutts

Illustrated by
David Rickman

Troll Associates

Library of Congress Cataloging in Publication Data

——

Jorinda and Joringel.

Summary: When a witch changes Jorinda into a
nightingale, her sweetheart Joringel discovers through
a dream how to save her.
[1. Fairy tales. 2. Folklore—Germany] I. Rickman,
David, ill. II. Grimm, Jacob, 1785-1863. Jorinde
und Joringel. III. Title.
PZ8.C96Jo 1988   398.2'1   [E]   87-10937
ISBN 0-8167-1065-1 (lib. bdg.)
ISBN 0-8167-1066-X (pbk.)

Copyright © 1988 by Troll Associates, Mahwah, N.J.

JORINDA AND JORINGEL

Once upon a time in a faraway land, there was a forest that was far more lovely and inviting than any other. When the sun was shining, the golden rays filtered down through the branches of the trees and painted beautiful patterns on the forest floor. The slightest breeze would set the leaves to singing, and the shadows seemed to dance in time to a happy tune. Because the forest was so lovely, people from the neighboring village often came to visit and stroll along its paths.

But deep in the forest was an enchanted castle that belonged to a witch. By day, the witch took the shape of a cat or a screech owl. By night, she changed herself back into human form again.

Whenever anyone came within a hundred paces of her castle, the witch would cast a spell. If a young man approached, he found that he could neither speak nor move until the witch released him from her spell. But if a maiden approached, the witch would turn her into a bird and put her into a wicker cage.

The witch had one room in the castle that was filled
with more than seven thousand cages. And in each cage
was a lovely bird that had once been a maiden.

Now it happened that one of the maidens in the nearby village was named Jorinda. She was more beautiful than anyone else, and was as sweet and kind as anyone could ever hope to be. In the same village there lived a handsome youth named Joringel, who loved Jorinda just as much as she loved him. One of the things they liked to do best was to wander down the paths of the forest, hand in hand, and talk about how happy they were. They were always careful to keep far away from the witch's castle.

One day, however, without realizing it, they wandered off the path and became lost in the forest. The late afternoon sunlight seemed to sparkle as it touched the flowers, and the birds sang happy songs. But Jorinda and Joringel felt strangely sad. Jorinda sat down and began to weep. Joringel looked around and for the first time saw that they were lost.

He peeked through the bushes, and what he saw
made the color drain from his face. There stood the
castle, its stone walls less than a hundred paces away.
For a moment, he could do nothing but stare. Then he
heard Jorinda's voice:

Everything I look upon
    Has turned from joy to sorrow;
My love will cry when I am gone,
    Tomorrow, morrow, morr—jug, jug!

Joringel turned toward her, but where Jorinda had been sitting there now stood a nightingale, singing, "jug, jug." The witch's spell had turned Jorinda into a bird. At that very moment, a screech owl flew out of the bushes. It flapped its wings and flew around the nightingale three times. Then its red eyes glared at Joringel, and its harsh voice rang out three times. Joringel suddenly realized that he could neither move nor speak. He was like a stone statue.

Then, just as the sun began to set, the owl flew back
into the bushes. A moment later, as the last rays of the sun
disappeared and night fell in the forest, a withered old
woman stepped out of the very place where the owl had
disappeared. Her crooked nose reached down almost to
the tip of her chin. Her eyes were as red as the screech
owl's, and Joringel knew at once that she was the witch.
She picked up the nightingale and went off toward the
castle. Joringel could do nothing but watch them go.

Some time later, the witch returned. She called out in a screeching voice, "When the moon shines into the castle and lights up the nightingale's cage, you will be set free."

A moment later, Joringel was free. He begged the
witch to return Jorinda to him, but she refused. Then he
fell to his knees and begged again and again, but nothing
he could say or do would make her change her mind.
"You shall never see her again," said the witch. "She is
mine—like all the others!" Then she cackled wickedly
and left him weeping in the forest.

Joringel became a shepherd in a nearby village. But he missed Jorinda so much that he often came into the forest and walked around the castle, hoping to catch sight of her. He was careful not to come too close, however, for he did not want to be turned into a statue again.

One night, Joringel had a dream that seemed almost real. In his dream, he found a special flower. Its petals were as red as blood and in its center was a huge white pearl. He picked the flower and went to the witch's castle. Whatever he touched with the flower was set free from the witch's enchantment.

When Joringel awoke, he remembered every detail of the dream. "Perhaps there is such a magic flower," he said. "If so, I must find it." And so he went out across the fields and forests, up the mountains and down the valleys, searching for a blood-red flower with a pearl at its center.

Early on the morning of the ninth day, he came upon a flower that was more beautiful than any other he had found so far. Its color was rich and deep, and in the center was an enormous drop of dew that looked for all the world like a glistening pearl.

Joringel picked the flower and headed straight for the witch's castle. He grew worried as he came within a hundred paces of the castle walls, but the flower kept him safe from the witch's spells.

He touched the door and it swung open. Then he walked down the halls of the castle and found the room with the wicker cages.

When he entered the room, he saw the witch. She was putting food into some of the cages, and cackling softly to herself. But when she saw Joringel, she flew into a rage. Her tongue dripped poison, and her eyes were like fire. Joringel paid no attention to her, but went from cage to cage, searching for the one that held Jorinda.

"How will I ever find her?" wondered Joringel. "There are so many cages, and the birds all look the same!" Just then, he saw the witch trying to sneak out the door, carrying a cage.

He ran up to her and touched the witch and the cage
with the magic flower. At once the witch lost her power,
and Jorinda stood where the nightingale's cage had been.

After that, he went from cage to cage, freeing all the other maidens who had been turned into birds by the wicked witch. And then Jorinda and Joringel went home to their village, where they were married, and lived happily for the rest of their lives.